New Paris
Grade School Library

# SPIT NOLAN

# SPIT NOLAN

## BILL NAUGHTON

Illustrated by
KATE BRENNAN HALL

CREATIVE EDUCATION, INC. MANKATO, MINNESOTA

Published by Creative Education, Inc. 123 South Broad Street,
Mankato, Minnesota 56001
Reprinted with the kind permission of Bill Naughton and
Thomas Nelson and Sons, Ltd., Surrey, England.

Copyright © 1988 by Creative Education, Inc.
International copyright reserved in all countries. No part of
this book may be reproduced in any form without written
permission from the publisher.
Printed in the United States of America.

**Library of Congress Cataloging-in-Publication Data**

Naughton, Bill.
Spit Nolan.

(Creative's classic short stories)

SUMMARY: A race between two coaster car
competitors in England ends tragically.

[1. Coaster cars — Fiction. 2. Racing — Fiction.
3. England — Fiction] I. Title. II. Series.
PZ7.N17475Sp   1987        [Fic]              87-5223
ISBN 0-88682-122-3
Mankato, MN: Creative Education: 32 p.

To the continuation and preservation
of short stories for readers
of all ages

Spit Nolan was a pal of mine. He was a thin lad with a bony face that was always pale, except for two rosy spots on his cheekbones. He had quick brown eyes, short, wiry hair, rather stooped shoulders, and we all knew that he had only one lung. He had had a disease which in those days couldn't be cured, unless you went away to Switzerland, which Spit certainly couldn't afford. He wasn't sorry for himself in any way, and in fact we envied him, because he never had to go to school.

Spit was the champion trolley-rider of Cotton Pocket; that was the district in which we lived. He had a very good balance, and sharp wits, and he was very brave, so that these qualities, when added to his skill as a rider, meant that no other boy could ever beat Spit on a trolley—and every lad had one.

  Our trolleys were simple vehicles for getting a good ride downhill at a fast speed. To make one you had to get a stout piece of wood about five feet in length and eighteen inches wide. Then you needed four wheels, preferably two pairs, large ones for the back and smaller ones for the front. However, since we bought our wheels from the scrapyard, most trolleys had four odd wheels. Now you had to get a poker and put it in the fire until it was red hot, and then burn a hole through the wood at the front. Usually it would take three or four attempts to get the hole bored through. Through this hole you fitted the giant nut-and-bolt, which acted as a swivel for the steering. Fastened to the nut was a strip of wood, on to which the front axle was secured by bent nails. A piece of rope tied to each end of the axle served for steering. Then a knob of margarine had to be slanced out of the kitchen to grease the wheels and bearings. Next you had to paint a name on it: *Invincible* or *Dreadnought,* though it might be a motto: *Death before Dishonor* or *Labour and Wait.* That done, you then stuck your chest out,

*Bill Naughton*

opened the back gate, and wheeled your trolley out to face the critical eyes of the world.

Spit spent most mornings trying out new speed gadgets on his trolley, or searching Enty's scrapyard for good wheels. Afternoons he would go off and have a spin down Cemetery Brew. This was a very steep road that led to the cemetery, and it was very popular with trolley-drivers as it was the only macadamised hill for miles around, all the others being cobblestones for horse traffic. Spit used to lie in wait for a coal-cart or other horse-drawn vehicle, then he would hitch *Egdam* to the back to take it up the brew. *Egdam* was a name in memory of a girl called Madge, whom he had once met at Southport Sanatorium, where he had spent three happy weeks. Only I knew the meaning of it, for he had reversed the letters of her name to keep his love a secret.

It was the custom for lads to gather at the street corner on summer evenings and, trolleys parked at hand, discuss trolleying, road surfaces, and also show off any new gadgets. Then, when Spit gave the sign, we used to set off for Cemetery Brew. There was scarcely any evening traffic on the roads in those days, so that we

*Spit Nolan*

could have a good practice before our evening race. Spit, the unbeaten champion, would inspect every trolley and rider, and allow a start which was reckoned on the size of the wheels and the weight of the rider. He was always the last in the line of starters, though no matter how long a start he gave it seemed impossible to beat him. He knew that road like the palm of his hand, every tiny lump or pothole, and he never came a cropper.

Among us he took things easy, but when occasion asked for it he would go all out. Once he had to meet a challenge from Ducker Smith, the champion of the Engine Row gang. On that occasion Spit borrowed a wheel from the baby's pram, removing one nearest the wall, so it wouldn't be missed, and confident he could replace it before his mother took baby out. And after fixing it to his trolley he made that ride on what was called the "belly-down" style—that is, he lay full stretch on his stomach, so as to avoid wind resistance. Although Ducker got away with a flying start he had not that sensitive touch of Spit, and his frequent bumps and swerves lost him valuable inches, so that he lost the race with a good three lengths. Spit arrived home just in time to catch his mother as she was wheeling young

*Spit Nolan*

Georgie off the doorstep, and if he had not made a dash for it the child would have fallen out as the pram overturned.

It happened that we were gathered at the street corner with our trolleys one evening when Ernie Haddock let out a hiccup of wonder: "Hy, chaps, wot's Leslie got?"

We all turned our eyes on Leslie Duckett, the plump son of the local publican. He approached us on a brand-new trolley, propelled by flicks of his foot on the pavement. From a distance the thing had looked impressive, but now, when it came up among us, we were too dumbfounded to speak. Such a magnificent trolley had never been seen! The riding board was of solid oak, almost two inches thick; four new wheels with pneumatic tires; a brake, a bell, a lamp, and a spotless steering-cord. In front was a plate on which was the name in bold lettering: *The British Queen.*

"It's called after the pub," remarked Leslie. He tried to edge it away from Spit's trolley, for it made *Egdam* appear horribly insignificant. Voices had been stilled for a minute, but now they broke out:

"Where'd it come from?"

"How much was it?"

*Spit Nolan*

"Who made it?"

Leslie tried to look modest. "My dad had it specially made to measure," he said, "by the gaffer of the Holt Engineering Works."

He was a nice lad, and now he wasn't sure whether to feel proud or ashamed. The fact was, nobody had ever had a trolley made by somebody else. Trolleys were swopped and so on, but no lad had ever owned one that had been made by other hands. We went quiet now, for Spit had calmly turned his attention to it, and was examining *The British Queen* with his expert eye. First he tilted it, so that one of the rear wheels was off the ground, and after giving it a flick of the finger he listened intently with his ear close to the hub.

"A beautiful ball-bearing race," he remarked, "it runs like silk." Next he turned his attention to the body. "Grand piece of timber, Leslie—though a trifle on the heavy side. It'll take plenty of pulling up a brew."

"I can pull it," said Leslie, stiffening.

"You might find it a shade *front-heavy*," went on Spit, "which means it'll be hard on the steering unless you keep it well oiled."

"It's well made," said Leslie. "Eh, Spit?"

Spit nodded. "Aye, all the bolts are counter-sunk," he said, "everything chamfered and fluted off to perfection. But—"

"But what?" asked Leslie.

"Do you want me to tell you?" asked Spit.

"Yes, I do," answered Leslie.

"Well, it's got none of *you* in it," said Spit.

"How do you mean?" says Leslie.

"Well, you haven't so much as given it a single tap with a hammer," said Spit. "That trolley will be a stranger to you to your dying day."

"How come," said Leslie, "since I *own* it?"

Spit shook his head, "You don't own it," he said, in a quiet, solemn tone. "You own nothing in this world except those things you have taken a hand in the making of, or else you've earned the money to buy them."

Leslie sat down on *The British Queen* to think this one out. We all sat round, scratching our heads.

"You've forgotten to mention one thing," said Ernie Haddock to Spit, "what about the *speed*?"

"Going down a steep hill," said Spit, "she should hold the road well—an' with wheels like that she should certainly be able to shift some."

"Think she could beat *Egdam*?" ventured Ernie.

"That," said Spit, "remains to be seen."

Ernie gave a shout: "A challenge race! *The British Queen* versus *Egdam*!"

"Not tonight," said Leslie. "I haven't got the proper feel of her yet."

"What about Sunday morning?" I said.

Spit nodded. "As good a time as any."

Leslie agreed. "By then," he said in a challenging tone, "I'll be able to handle her."

Chattering like monkeys, eating bread, carrots, fruit, and bits of toffee, the entire gang of us made our way along the silent Sunday-morning streets for the big race at Cemetery Brew. We were split into two fairly equal sides.

Leslie, in his serge Sunday suit, walked ahead, with Ernie Haddock pulling *The British Queen,* and a bunch of supporters around. They were optimistic, for Leslie had easily outpaced every other trolley during the week, though as yet he had not run against Spit.

Spit was in the middle of the group behind, and I was pulling *Egdam* and keeping the pace easy, for I

## Spit Nolan

wanted Spit to keep fresh. He walked in and out among us with an air of imperturbability that, considering the occasion, seemed almost godlike. It inspired a fanatical confidence in us. It was such that Chick Dale, a curly-headed kid with soft skin like a girl's, and a nervous lisp, climbed up on to the spiked railings of the cemetery, and, reaching out with his thin fingers, snatched a yellow rose. He ran in front of Spit and thrust it into a small hole in his jersey.

"I pwesent you with the wose of the winner!" he exclaimed.

"And I've a good mind to present you with a clout on the lug," replied Spit, "for pinching a flower from a cemetery. An' what's more, it's bad luck." Seeing Chick's face, he relented. "On second thoughts, Chick, I'll wear it. Ee, wot a 'eavenly smell!"

Happily we went along, and Spit turned to a couple of lads at the back. "Hy, stop that whistling. Don't forget what day it is—folk want their sleep out."

A faint sweated glow had come over Spit's face when we reached the top of the hill, but he was as majestically calm as ever. Taking the bottle of cold water from his trolley seat, he put it to his lips and rinsed out his mouth in the manner of a boxer.

The two contestants were called together by Ernie.

"No bumpin' or borin'," he said.

They nodded.

"The winner," he said, "is the first who puts the nose of his trolley past the cemetery gates."

They nodded.

"Now, who," he asked, "is to be judge?"

Leslie looked at me. "I've no objection to Bill," he said. "I know he's straight."

I hadn't realised I was, I thought, but by heck I will be!

"Ernie here," said Spit, "can be starter."

With that Leslie and Spit shook hands.

"Fly down to them gates," said Ernie to me. He had his father's pigeon-timing watch in his hand. "I'll be setting 'em off dead on the stroke of ten o'clock."

I hurried down to the gates. I looked back and saw the supporters lining themselves on either side of the road. Leslie was sitting upright on *The British Queen*. Spit was settling himself to ride belly-down. Ernie Haddock, handkerchief raised in the right hand, eye gazing down on the watch in the left, was counting them off—just like when he tossed one of his father's pigeons.

*Bill Naughton*

"Five—four—three—two—one—*Off!*"

Spit was away like a shot. That vigorous toe push sent him clean ahead of Leslie. A volley of shouts went up from his supporters, and groans from Leslie's. I saw Spit move straight to the middle of the road camber. Then I ran ahead to take up my position at the winning-post.

When I turned again I was surprised to see that Spit had not increased the lead. In fact, it seemed that Leslie had begun to gain on him. He had settled himself into a crouched position, and those perfect wheels combined with his extra weight were bringing him up with Spit. Not that it seemed possible he could ever catch him. For Spit, lying flat on his trolley, moving with a fine balance, gliding, as it were, over the rough patches, looked to me as though he were a bird that might suddenly open out its wings and fly clean into the air.

The runners along the side could no longer keep up with the trolleys. And now, as they skimmed past the half-way mark, and came to the very steepest part, there was no doubt that Leslie was gaining. Spit had never ridden better; he coaxed *Egdam* over the tricky parts, swayed with her, gave her her head, and guided

*Spit Nolan*

her. Yet Leslie, clinging grimly to the steering-rope of *The British Queen*, and riding the rougher part of the road, was actually drawing level. Those beautiful ball-bearing wheels, engineer-made, encased in oil, were holding the road, and bringing Leslie along faster than spirit and skill could carry Spit.

Dead level they sped into the final stretch. Spit's slight figure was poised fearlessly on his trolley, drawing the extremes of speed from her. Thundering beside him, anxious but determined, came Leslie. He was actually drawing ahead—and forcing his way to the top of the camber. On they came like two charioteers—Spit delicately edging to the side, to gain inches by the extra downward momentum. I kept my eyes fastened clean across the road as they came belting past the winning-post.

First past was the plate *The British Queen*. I saw that first. Then I saw the heavy rear wheel jog over a pothole and strike Spit's front wheel—sending him in a swerve across the road. Suddenly then, from nowhere, a charabanc* came speeding round the wide bend.

Spit was straight in its path. Nothing could avoid the collision. I gave a cry of fear as I saw the heavy solid tire of the front wheel hit the trolley. Spit was flung up

*A large bus, often used for sightseeing

and his back hit the radiator. Then the driver stopped dead.

I got there first. Spit was lying on the macadam road on his side. His face was white and dusty, and coming out between his lips and trickling down his chin was a rivulet of fresh red blood. Scattered all about him were yellow rose petals.

"Not my fault," I heard the driver shouting. "I didn't have a chance. He came straight at me."

The next thing we were surrounded by women who had got out of the charabanc. And then Leslie and all the lads came up.

"Somebody send for an ambulance!" called a woman.

"I'll run an' tell the gatekeeper to telephone," said Ernie Haddock.

"I hadn't a chance," the driver explained to the woman.

"A piece of his jersey on the starting-handle there..." said someone.

"Don't move him," said the driver to a stout woman who had bent over Spit. "Wait for the ambulance."

"Hush up," she said. She knelt and put a silk scarf under Spit's head. Then she wiped his mouth with her

little handkerchief.

He opened his eyes. Glazed they were, as though he couldn't see. A short cough came out of him, then he looked at me and his lips moved.

"*Who won?*"

"Thee!" blurted out Leslie. "Tha just licked me. Eh, Bill?"

"Aye," I said, "old *Egdam* just pipped *The British Queen*."

Spit's eyes closed again. The women looked at each other. They nearly all had tears in their eyes. Then Spit looked up again, and his wise, knowing look came over his face. After a minute he spoke in a sharp whisper:

"Liars. I can remember seeing Leslie's back wheel hit my front 'un. I didn't win—I lost." He stared upward for a few seconds, then his eyes twitched and shut.

The driver kept repeating how it wasn't his fault, and next thing the ambulance came. Nearly all the women were crying now, and I saw the look that went between the two men who put Spit on a stretcher—but I couldn't believe he was dead. I had to go into the ambulance with the attendant to give him particulars. I went up the step and sat down inside and looked out the little window as the driver slammed the doors. I saw the driver holding Leslie as a witness. Chick Dale was lifting the smashed-up *Egdam* on to the body of *The British Queen*. People with bunches of flowers in their hands stared after us as we drove off. Then I heard the ambulance man asking me Spit's name. Then he touched me on the elbow with his pencil and said:

"Where *did* he live?"

I knew then. That word "did" struck right into me. But for a minute I couldn't answer. I had to think hard, for the way he said it made it suddenly seem as though Spit Nolan had been dead and gone for ages.

*Bill Naughton*

Bill Naughton is an English author and playwright who was born in Ireland. His family moved to England, however, and he spent his youth in Lancashire where his father was a coal miner. Naughton has used, and continues to use, this coal mining country as the setting for his plays and stories. Naughton also uses personal experiences with family and friends in his writing.

Naughton has worked at other jobs besides writing. He worked for a time as a laborer, lorry driver, weaver, coalbagger, and bleacher. He has used his experiences in these jobs to enhance his writing and add to his characters and plots.

Naughton's characters are realistic, often tenderly presented. His characters which are children are typical of Naughton and his childhood pals.

Although many people know him for his books, Naughton has written numerous plays for the stage, radio and television.

Naughton's works have earned him honors including Screenwriters Guild Awards, Prix Italia, and Other Award from Children's Rights Workshop.

*This book was designed by Bill Foster and typeset by House of Graphics, St. Paul, Minnesota.*

*It is typeset in English Times.*

*The color separations were done by The John Roberts Printing Company, Minneapolis, Minnesota.*

*Worzalla Publishing Company, Stevens Point, Wisconsin did the printing and binding.*

F
NAU
Naughton, Bill

SPIT NOLAN

MAY 89

**DATE DUE**

| | | | |
|---|---|---|---|
| | | | |
| | | | |
| | | | |
| | | | |
| | | | |
| | | | |
| | | | |
| | | | |
| | | | |
| | | | |

New Paris
Grade School Library